Ned's Noise Machine

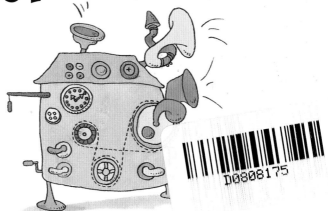

Monica Hughes

Illustrated by Serena Feneziani

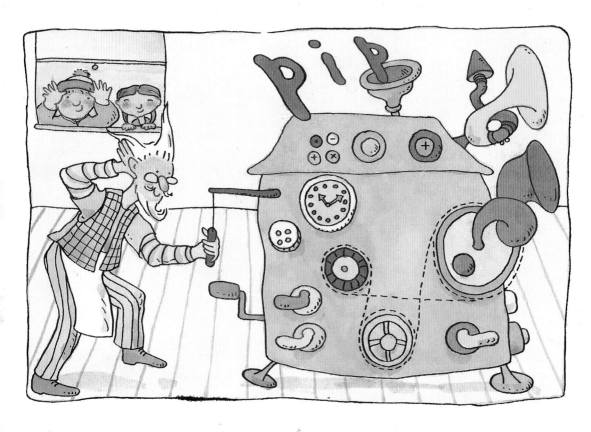

It can go pip.

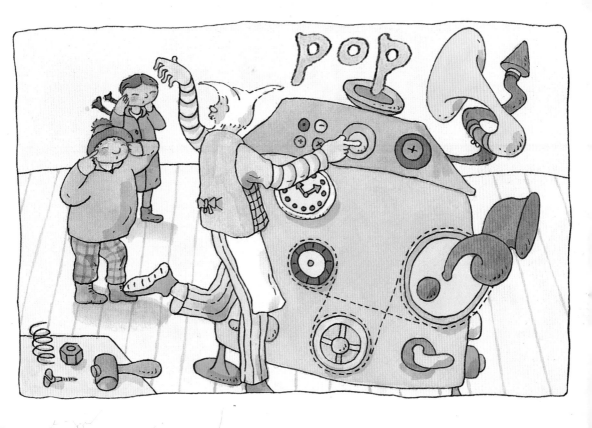

It can go pop.

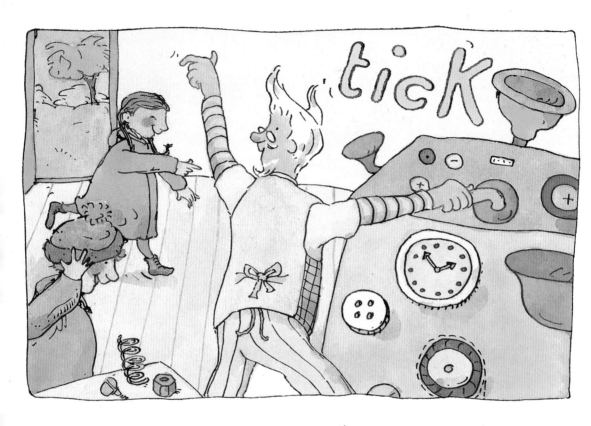

It can go tick.

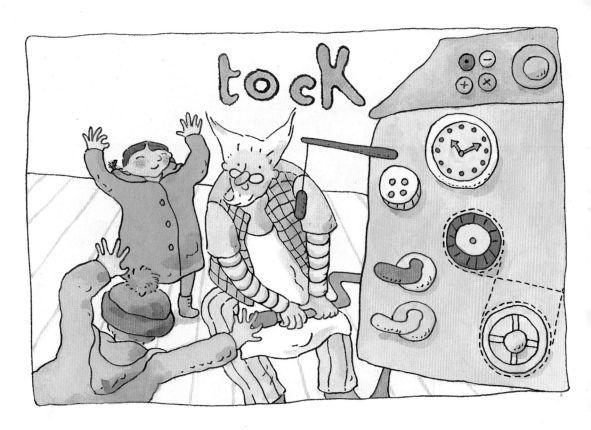

It can go tock.

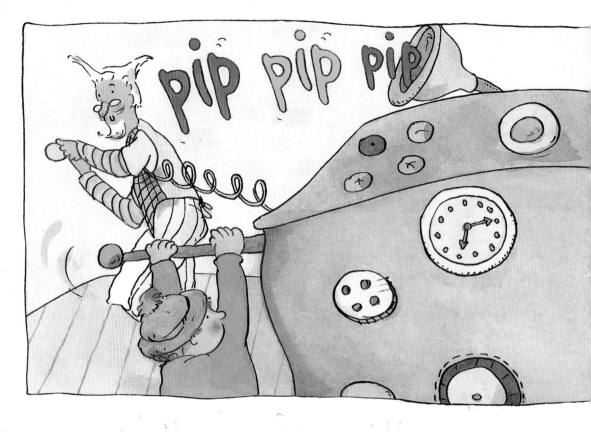

It can go pip, pip, pip.

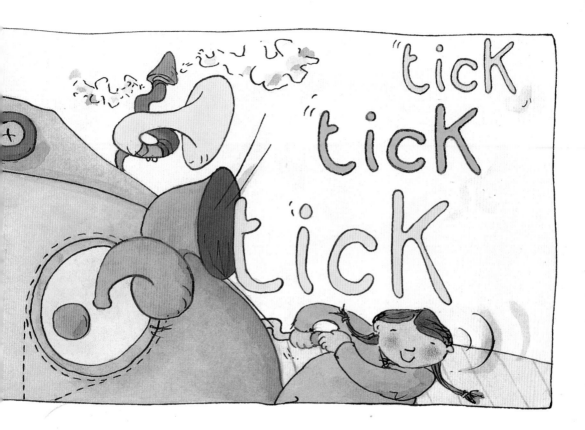

It can go tick, tick, tick.

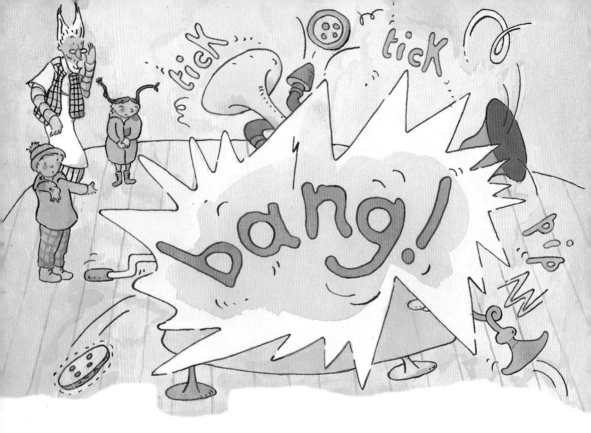

It can go bang!